THE ARRANGEMENT

Vol. 8

H.M. Ward

www.SexyAwesomeBooks.com

Laree Bailey Press

COPYRIGHT

Laree Bailey Press
First Edition: August 2013
ISBN: 978-0615860824

CHAPTER 1

I'm pacing the floor of the hotel room, fuming. How could Sean say that? My fingers ball into fists, as I kick off each shoe and watch them fly across the room. *Do whatever you want*, he said. Damn right that I'm going to do whatever I want. Moving through the room quickly, I start packing my things, shoving them into the bag. The urge to scream has been building inside of me since dinner. It wasn't Peter or Sidney— it was Sean.

I had my fork halfway to my mouth when Sean announced that he was leaving and heading out with Peter for a few days. When I first heard the news, I could only manage to blink at Sean. He didn't invite me along, he didn't tell me he was leaving, and the words he said made me so goddamn angry that I stormed away from the table like some sort of deranged drama queen—but I couldn't sit there anymore. I would have smashed my plate over his head.

Sean watched me walk away and did nothing to stop me. He didn't chase after me or call out for me to stop. He let me walk away without even glancing my way. There was no concern, no remorse. *Do whatever you want.*

I step into the bathroom, and try to grab all my stuff in one trip. I pile my make-up bag and hair stuff into my arms, and head to the shower to grab my conditioner. When I lean forward, everything tumbles out of my arms and skitters across the floor. I stand there for a moment and stare. This isn't happening to me. It's not real. I'll go home later and Mom will be there. She can fix this.

She would have been able to…

My throat tightens to the point that I can't swallow. My gaze blurs as my thoughts take off in a million different directions like dandelion seeds in the wind. I don't hear Sean standing behind me until he speaks.

"What are you doing?" His voice is deep, demanding.

I don't turn. My body remains rigid, with my shoulders too tense. If he touches me, I'll punch him. Anger is swirling inside of me and mixing with dread. Things can't end this way.

Something inside me snaps and I round on him. Before Sean can speak, I slam my open palms into his chest, shoving him as hard as I can. Sean barely moves. It's like I'm no more substantial than a snowflake.

"What am *I* doing? Me? You're asking me? How about *you*? What the hell are you doing?" Sean doesn't answer, so I slam my hands into his chest again, harder this time. "Tell me! Don't just stand there like that and act like nothing's wrong!"

When my hands slam into his chest again, Sean grabs hold of my wrists and doesn't let go. He yanks me toward him so my face is close to his. "I have no idea what you're talking about or why you behaved as you did downstairs."

I lean back, trying to pull away from him, but Sean won't let me. "You know exactly what you did down there! You knew what would happen before you even said it—I could see it on your face—so don't you dare lie to me now, and act like you have no idea why I'm mad. And, I swear to God, if you blame it on PMS, I will cut you."

Sean represses a smirk at my threat. His blue gaze seems amused by the idea, as if I could possibly hurt him. The man is made of stone. Nothing hurts him, not anymore. "As delightful as it sounds to see you in a full blown rage, I hardly think your behavior is warranted."

"You handed me off to Henry," I hiss. "Don't play this game with me Sean. Don't stand there and pretend that you didn't. You're leaving me tomorrow and you didn't say a damn thing about it."

"I didn't hand you off to anyone. You made your own decision and I made mine." Sean drops my wrists, like he's through with me, and walks out of the bathroom. He crosses the floor and pulls a bottle of liquor out of the bar. Everything about him is so calm, like nothing is wrong. He pours his drink as I stare at him in disbelief.

"What decision did I make, Sean? Because I don't remember making one that included you leaving New York without me."

"This is childish, Avery. We're both adults here." Sean turns toward me and leans back against the bar. The tumbler is loosely held in his hand, and everything about the way he stands says he doesn't care. "And I did not hand you off to Henry Thomas. You chose him when you failed to choose me."

"That's what this is about? Are you insane? I didn't choose Henry."

"You didn't choose me, did you? Or did I miss something?" Sean raises the glass to his lips and tips it back. The contents disappear in one gulp. Sean glances up at me from under his brow, waiting for an answer. My jaw is open and I hesitate. The words are there, but I can't say them. I don't want to hurt him. A smug expression spreads across Sean's face. "I thought so."

Fuck it. I stomp over to him and look up into his beautiful face. "You thought what? You thought that I'd be happy to be your live-in call girl? You thought that I'd be flattered that you offered to buy me?"

"I offered you more than that and you know it." Sean sets down his empty glass firmly, and folds his arms over his chest as his eyes narrow into slits, like he's ready to fight. Everything about him says that I should back off, that there is no way to win this argument, but I can't shut up.

Rage is coursing through my veins so rapidly that I want to strangle him. "Did you? Because I didn't hear that. You said that you wouldn't share, that I'd be yours. You said you loved me and then you offered to buy me from Black. What the fuck am I supposed to do with that—be flattered? Swoon, fall at your feet, and thank you for hiring me to be your own personal sex slave. Wake up, Sean!"

Sean moves quickly. Suddenly his face is a breath from mine. "I offered to take care of you. I offered for you to be with me and you said no."

"I did not."

"You didn't accept."

"How could I?" The rapid exchange of biting words stops. We stare at each other a beat too long.

Sean tears his gaze away from mine and turns his back on me. He places his hands on the bar and hangs his head like this is impossible. "What more do you want from me, Avery?"

The moment feels fragile, like I'm stepping out onto a frozen lake that's nearly thawed. I reach for him, but hesitate. I don't touch his shoulder like I want. Instead, I say the words to his back. "I want everything. There is no in the middle, not for me. We can't date for a while and try things out because of my job. You know that. It's all or nothing."

Sean glances over his shoulder at me with confusion pinching his face. "You want to marry me?"

The way he says it, like marriage is the last thing he'd ever do, crushes me. I hide the emotions before he sees them. I mask the way his words crush me one by one, but the truth is already on my lips and I'm telling him what I want before I can stop. "I want the little house with the hanging baskets full of flowers on the front porch. I want my office inside, so that I can be home with the kids. I want a big fluffy dog that digs up my roses, and I want the husband who kisses me on the cheek when he comes home. I know what I want Sean, and being a mistress doesn't fit into it at all."

"I see." His gaze is locked with mine. Too many moments pass with words unsaid. The pit of my stomach grows colder and colder. It's like I can sense him pulling away. My dreams aren't his dreams. I can see it on his face. "And being a call girl does?"

"It's temporary."

He nods and his gaze falls to the floor. "I don't have more to offer."

I smile sadly at him. "Your offer wasn't good enough, not for me. I can't accept it no matter how I feel about you. I'm sorry Sean."

CHAPTER 2

Sean nods, like he already knows. He glances up at me. "So, you're back to being my call girl?"

I hate that he gives up so easily. If Sean gave even the faintest hint that we might end up together, my words would be different. But he doesn't. I steel myself so that my answer comes out smooth and sure. "If that's the best you can offer, then yes."

Sean steps toward me and laces his hands around my waist. "I can't do forever, Avery."

"So," I swallow hard. This feels like good-bye, like I'll never see him again. The thought of not seeing him is too much. I push it away and manage to tug my lips into a slight smile. "So, tell me what you want tonight, Mr. Jones. I'm yours until morning." The words sound light, but they fall out of the air like stones.

Sean works his jaw and watches me for a moment before answering. His eyes burn with words that I've never heard him say. I wonder if it's real, or if I imagined how much he loves me. Thoughts like that won't help, not now.

Sean tips his head forward, so it's resting against mine. "I'll tell you what I want, what I intend to do with you, Miss Smith." There's no remorse in his voice, no indication that he hates this as much as I do. I bet his mind is already some place dark, ready to tie me up again. I repress the urge to shiver as I think about it. Dinner was rough and this moment doesn't make it better. No doubt, Sean plans on giving me a serious mind fuck as a going away present.

Sean dips his hands lower, cupping my butt and pulling us closer together. His lips are by my ear, his breath tickling me as he speaks. "I'm going to make love to you, Avery. You are going to be so sated that you'll never be able to have sex again without thinking about this night. I promise you that."

Surprised, I say, "I thought—"

"I know." He kisses the top of my head, giving me the gentle touches that I so desperately crave. "I don't want our last time together to be like that."

I knew it was true before he said the sentence, but it still hits me like a two by four. "So, you're leaving—after you help Peter—you'll go back to California?"

"I've overstayed my visit, Avery. I should have left weeks ago." Sean's fingers press into my back as he slides them up to the zipper. He pulls it down and pushes the dress off my shoulders. The fabric slips down between us, pooling at my waist.

Sean and I stare at each other. Every reservation I have about his offer is fighting within me. I try to make a logical argument for accepting, but I can't. I have years of schooling left and if something happens—if we break up—then I'll be back in the spot I am now. At least this way I get to control my life. I know I'm too softhearted to live this way for very long. I know it'll destroy me, but I still can't walk away from it.

When I was a child, I pictured a guy that would come along and sweep me off my feet. He'd want to take care of me and make me smile. He'd want to be there for me on any terms he could get.

Sean isn't that guy—he just isn't.

I know I have to let him go, even though I don't want to. Whatever weird-ass relationship we had is over, and this is the last time I'll be with him. As the thought solidifies, it feels like I've been buried under an avalanche of stone. I can't breathe. Tears prick the back of my eyes, but they don't fall. I wish I was numb. I wish I could say yes to him. I wish I had a different life, because this one is so horrendously unfair.

Sean pulls me from my downward spiral of thoughts. He touches my cheek and leans in, kissing me softly. I close my eyes and decide to lose myself in his arms one last time. There's no point in holding back, is there? He already knows how I feel about him, it's not like holding back will hide anything.

The thoughts slip from my mind as his mouth drifts over my cheek and down my neck. He presses his hot lips to my skin over and over again, each time softer than that last. The gentle kisses make my eyelids flutter closed. I sigh, contented, and thread my fingers through his hair. Each kiss is perfect and teasing.

Sean lingers, slowly working his way from one side of my neck to the other. I tilt my head back, rolling it to the side, as the kisses become longer. He finds the spot at the base of my neck that makes me melt. Brushing his lips against my skin, Sean teases me before pressing his mouth harder against my skin, increasing the pressure. His tongue sweeps over that spot and every single rational thought flies from my mind.

A moan escapes from me after a moment and my knees give out. I slip against his hard chest, but Sean doesn't stop. He holds me tightly against him, kissing the spot harder and more passionately. I shudder in his arms as a myriad of sensations shoot through me.

Since I've been with him, I learned there are a few, very small, highly sensitive spots on my body and when they're touched the right way, it's euphoric bliss. Sean works the spot with his tongue, never stopping, pressing harder. My eyelids feel so heavy, but the rest of my body feels light and tingly. Part of me wants to hold on, to remain aware of my surroundings, to be coherent and careful.

Sean senses my apprehension. He lifts his lips from my neck and whispers in my ear, "Let go, Avery."

"I can't…" My voice is barely there. It catches in the back of my throat before it comes out. I want to let go, I want to—I just can't. Out of all the things we've done, he's not been like this before. I'm breathing so hard.

"You can. Trust me, baby. I'll take care of you. Let go, let everything else fade away." As Sean speaks, his voice becomes deeper and more unguarded.

He presses his lips lightly to that spot again, and I keep thinking that this will be the last time. There won't be more Sean. There won't be another chance to lie in each other's arms and make love. At the same time, the idea of losing myself in him—of completely giving myself over to him—scares me. Fear holds me back.

It's several moments before Sean speaks again. "I love you, Avery. I always will…" He doesn't say anything else. He doesn't pressure me to let go, to lose control. He continues to kiss me, softly, as my mind reels.

I want this. The words echo over and over again. His words, and then his lips, push me over the edge of reason. Something inside of me, the part of my mind that so desperately tries to keep me in one piece, disappears and I'm left alone with Sean.

Desire courses through me, swirling in my stomach, and then shooting between my legs. I dig my nails into his shirt, wishing it wasn't there. My head tips back and I moan his name.

Sean presses me into the wall, using his body to hold me in place. My fingers play with his hair, as Sean dips his head and trails kisses from my neck to my breast. I'm saying things, things that sound too carnal to be coming from my mouth, urging him on. Sean pushes the strap of my bra down and frees my tender flesh. My nipples are taut, craving contact with his lips, but he doesn't do that. Instead, he touches me gently, moving his hand over my breast before rubbing his thumb over my nipple. I suck in air and slam back into the wall.

Everything feels more intense than usual. Each place his fingers touch flames to life. My hips buck against his as Sean crushes me into the wall. I can feel how much he wants me through his slacks. I wish he'd take them off. I lick my lips, thinking about taking him in my mouth, about tasting him.

While my eyes are closed and my mind is lost in lust, Sean takes my breast in his mouth. The response is instant and I can't remain silent. I gasp, saying his name as my stomach flips, and take his head between my hands. Tangling my fingers in his dark hair,

I hold him there against me, urging him to suck, lick, and taste me—to do anything and everything he wants. Waves of lust swirl inside of me, filling my body, until I'm consumed by them. They demand things, and urge me on, making me say things I'd never say in the light of day.

But things are different here, with him, now. There's a connection between us, like we were made for each other. I feel it, something within me calls to him, wants him, and needs him. It's like his name was written on my soul and he belongs to me, and in this moment he does. In this moment, Sean is mine.

When his mouth moves, his kisses change from gentle to demanding. His tongue swirls around my nipple, flicking and sucking it. Every time he does this, I slip down the wall, unable to stand on my own. Sean presses into me, holding me in place. He works my sensitive flesh until I'm floating so high from lust that I don't want to come down, but the place between my legs is throbbing, demanding attention.

Sean knows what he's done to me, what I'm craving. Before more filthy suggestions fly out of my mouth, his hand slips between my legs and around the scrap of fabric covering me. As his lips work my breast, his finger pushes into me—once—fast and hard. I gasp as he does it and suddenly feel all those tightly wound coils break free. Clawing his back, I buck against his hand, moaning, as I come.

Sean lifts his head from my breast and watches me as my hips rock against his palm. My gaze is heavy with longing, but I'm aware he's watching me. I slip my tongue over my lips slowly and blink at him, like I want more.

A wicked smile spreads across his lips. "One, you naughty woman."

A satisfied smile crosses my lips. "Are we counting?"

"We won't need to. You'll remember how many times you came tonight and exactly what we were doing." Sean leans in and nips my neck. I grin, unable to hide how I feel. "I need to fuck you senseless before you wake up from the slutty state you're floating in, beautiful woman."

Before he finishes speaking, Sean scoops me up in his arms and carries me across the room. He pulls the sofa chair into the middle of the floor with his foot and then bends me over the edge. My dress is still around my hips, my bra is half on, half off, and the G string around my bottom is quickly removed. Sean unzips his pants and then leans on me. I can feel how much he wants me, which makes me gasp.

"Oh my God, you're perfect. You know that, right?" Sean rubs his hands over my back, before he sits up and slips his fingers between the V in my legs.

I try to answer him, but I can only make noises in the back of my throat. I'm so wet that his fingers slide easily inside of me. I rock against his hand, pushing back and wanting more, wanting him. He holds me there like that, bent over with my bare ass facing him. After a few moments, I realize he's teasing me and only touching the sensitive nub. As he does it, I gasp and beg for him to do more. I can't take the torment.

"Please, Sean, oh God, please fuck me. Please, baby…" His fingers squeeze me hard before slipping into the right spot and disappearing inside of me. I cry out as he pushes a finger in and out of me, making me hotter than I was before, but not offering me any release. My breasts rub against the chair, which makes me completely crazy.

I need him inside of me, but he waits. Instead, the fingers on his other hand trail the curves of my body, lightly touching and caressing every rise and fall of naked flesh. His eyes devour me. Hot breath washes over my neck as his hand moves over my body while the other rocks in and out of me.

The tender touches make me want to turn around and straddle him. Every part of me is humming, begging to be ridden, wanting to feel him inside of me. The light touch of his hands, and the teasing movements between my legs, makes me throw my head back and pant. The air feels hot and thick. My body is covered in sweat, my dress is wrinkled around my hips, and I don't care about anything except having him inside of me, banging into me over and over again. I want him so badly that I can't control myself anymore.

I'm begging him, "Please, Sean… Baby, please."

I say it again and again, each time pushing my hips harder against his hand. I can feel his dick against my thigh and wish he'd take me. I want him, I need to feel his long, hard length inside of me, rocking and slamming into me. I beg him again, saying anything that comes to mind, anything at all, to try and make him fuck me.

Sean's voice sounds light when he speaks, as if he's enjoying my slutty state more than I am. "Tell me what you want, baby."

"Be with me, Sean. Please, please, please…" I beg again, not thinking about what it means or looks like. I'll do anything to have him right then and he knows it.

"I am with you, Avery." He leans over and presses his back against me, taking a fist full of my breast in his hand. He squeezes me, and rubs my nipple gently. My hips involuntarily buck against him. "You'll have to be more specific, beautiful."

"Fuck me." My voice is shaking and breathy when I say it, when I beg him.

"You want me to fuck you, baby?" I nod vigorously and look over my shoulder, waiting and hoping that he'll take me. "Tell me how much you want it. Tell me how badly you want my dick."

"I need you, baby. I want your dick so much, more than anything else. I want to feel how hard and sharp you are when you push inside of me. I want it, Sean. I need you to fuck me. I need it so much. Please, baby, please. Fuck me hard. Take me. Please, Sean…" My begging becomes frantic as I try to think of what else I can say to convince him how much I want to be with him.

Sean shifts against me, hard and ready. I must have said the right thing, because he slips his fingers out of me and shifts his hips. I feel him brush against me and then he pushes in so slowly that it's all I can manage to stay still.

The insane desire to ride him like a pogo stick rushes through me and I can't help it—I push back against him, slamming my hips into his, and forcing him deep inside of me quickly. A high pitched sound comes from my throat as I buck against him over and over.

Sean has me so close to the edge that a breeze would make me come, and I do.

Wildly, I slam my hips back against him, as waves of pleasure course through me. I'm spent, breathless and leaning over the edge of the bench.

Sean continues to rock into me, slowly, firmly, and then pulls out. His fingers lightly touch my back and I don't realize what he's doing until his lips are on my skin. There's a spot on my back, just under my shoulder, that is as sensitive as the one on my neck. It's like my body came equipped with slut buttons that I never knew were there. Sean seems to know. He pushes himself in and out, slowly, and when his lips come down on that spot on my back, I nearly jerk upright.

That touch, the way it feels, is so charged that I can't sit still. Sean presses me down, stilling me, and continues to work the spot with his lips and then his tongue. My mind is completely gone, it floats away and doesn't come back. Desperation shoots through me when I feel the need to be ridden, again.

My heart races harder and faster as Sean works his magic, pushing buttons that I didn't know I had. I cry out as my fingernails dig into the fabric on the pillow in front of me. Sean pushes a finger between my legs and up inside of me.

He purrs in my ear as he breathes deeply. His hand moves faster, as he kisses my back. By the time he stops to fuck me, I'm someone else. My body is on fire, demanding his dick, wanting him pounding into me. And he does, oh God, he does. Sean takes hold of my hips and pushes in so hard and deep. Then he does it again, and again, until he's riding me so roughly that it should hurt, but it doesn't. I want him like this, and I want more.

As the sensations build within me, I climb higher and higher. Needing release, I scream as I buck into him too many times to count, and I finally shatter. Gasping, I cry out and he pushes into me once, hard. Breathless, I lean there, unable to move, and listen to him moan. His fingers are clutching my hips and I feel more sated than I have ever felt in my life. I can barely breathe, and I notice how wet we are, but I don't think he came. I glance back at him and ask.

There's a sultry smile on his face. Sean leans forward and kisses me. "Not yet, baby.

That was you." It takes a moment for it to sink in—I came and he's soaked? I did that? Before embarrassment hits me in the head like a frying pan, Sean says, "And it was the sexiest thing I've ever seen. I want to take you over to the bed and lick you until you come in my mouth. Oh my God, Avery. Do you have any idea how sexy you are? It's like you're a goddess sent here to torment me."

Sean pulls away and then turns me toward him. He strips the rest of my clothes before carrying me over to the bed. He sets me down and fans my hair around my head before asking, "Ready for more, Miss Smith?"

I grin, I can't help it. I want more. "Always."

CHAPTER 3

Sean and I part ways in the early hours of the morning. As he packs up his things, it hits me hard. I manage to smile and say good-bye without crying. I keep thinking that Sean will offer something more, but he doesn't. His blue eyes avoid mine, like he's sorry this didn't work out.

I wish I could stay, I wish I could say yes, but I can't.

"So this is it, then?" I'm standing next to the door with my bag over my shoulder as I strangle the handle on my suitcase. I swear to God, it's going to crack in my fist. I hate this, but I chose it. Things are over and I'm the one who ended them. I smile at him, like I'm fine with it, even though I'd rather shove glass shards into my eyeballs.

"I guess so." Sean stops packing and struts over to the door. The black dress shirt he's wearing is open, revealing his beautiful chest. My eyes wander to his abs and linger too long. "My eyes are up here, Smitty." I glance up to find him smiling at me. Sean closes the distance between us and takes me in his arms. He kisses my cheek and releases me.

I don't know what to say to fill the silence. I don't know how to fix this. It seems wrong to leave him, but I have to. There's no compromise, no alternative. Things just weren't meant to be, which seems like a pansy-ass thing to say, until it happens to you.

My mind is reeling, trying to figure out something else, but there isn't anything else. Sean came into town and now it's over. I manage, "Call me next time you're in New York."

He nods once and reaches for the doorknob. As he pulls it open, Sean says, "I will. Take care of yourself, Avery." Our eyes lock and the pit of my stomach drops. I want to lean into him, I want his arms to wrap around me and hold me tight—but none of those things happen.

"Right back at you, Motorcycle Man." My voice picks up a quiver and I know that I can't linger without busting a hole in my tear ducts. They feel swollen under my face, like I'll flood the whole damn island if I don't get out of there. I step through the door and walk down the hallway without looking back.

It's the last time I'll see Sean Ferro. I'm certain of it.

———

By the time Gabe drops me off at the dorm, it's nearly seven in the morning. It's Sunday, which means Amber is probably sound asleep. I walk down the quiet halls feeling like there's an anvil on my chest. Sean isn't the guy for me. He doesn't want what I want. We're too incompatible, so why am I upset? It's better that I found out now. It has to be, right?

Gabe told me to get some rest and that he'd be back for me later this afternoon. I can't even imagine faking my way through being with Henry. The whole situation is too much. I slip into my room and trip over something in the darkness. My emotions are so frayed that I can't stop the rush of expletives that are cascading from my mouth.

Amber yells at me and flicks on the light next to her bed. "Holy shit, Avery. Could you be any louder?" I glance at her. Amber is sitting up with a sheet clutched against her naked chest with too much boob poking out for me to look at her.

I glance down to see what I tripped on—shoes. I stare at them for a moment and then look up wide-eyed. "No, no, no. Tell me you didn't—"

"I was lonely and he was—" Amber's shoulders rise until they swallow her neck and she gives me a sheepish look.

A male voice finishes her sentence. "Utterly fuckable. Yeah, I am." Naked Guy walks past me in his birthday suit, which makes my eye twitch. "Hey roomie, nice dress."

"He can't stay here." My brain is melting. I feel it boil over and leak out of my ears. I don't have the patience for this. I don't. In the calmest voice I can muster, I manage, "Amber, so help me God, he needs to leave right now or I'll—"

Naked Guy slips into bed next to Amber and grins at me. "Take a chill pill, little lady. I was just showing my friend Amber a good time. I'd be happy to let you take a ride on Giant when we're done. Yeah, I named him Giant, because there's no point to calling him Little, right, Amber?"

Amber has a goofy smile on her face. I feel like I'm her mother, not her roommate, which rubs me wrong. My left eye twitches as I stare at her, waiting for her to toss him out, but she doesn't.

"Of course," I mutter and shake my head. I disappear into our tiny bathroom and change as fast as I can.

It's the buttcrack of dawn and I'm so not dealing with them right now. I slip on a pair of sneakers and glance at the purple coat Sean bought me. I grab it and dart out the door. As I head down the hallway, I ram straight into Mel.

We smack together before I realize it's her. "I'm sorry… Oh, hey. Late night?"

Mel nods after shaking off the irritation of being bumped. It's like Mel can't fathom someone not seeing her. Right then I wasn't seeing anyone because I had Naked Guy burned into the back of my eyelids. Gross.

"Yeah, just getting back. Where are you headed?"

"Out of here. Naked Guy is back and I don't want to witness the bumping of uglies. There's enough ugly in my room already. I'm going to grab breakfast and sit at the dock or something until my client later today."

Mel nods slowly, like she's waiting for me to elaborate, but I don't. She folds her arms over her pretty dress and cocks her head to the side. "You want to talk about it?"

"No. It's a job, Mel. In fact, I'm signing on with Black for more contracts when I see her later."

Mel's golden eyes narrow like she knows that I'm not telling her something. "Yeah, and what about Ferro?"

"He left town, so it's not like he'll be booking me again." My voice catches in the back of my throat. "Asking for more clients is a good thing, right? I mean, that way I can set aside some money before finals come. I was hoping not to work much the last few weeks of school."

Mel nods. "Maybe—but Avery, do me a favor and take it slow. You don't need to fuck Manhattan to get over him."

"Sean asked me to stay with him," I don't look at her as I say it. Instead, I twist the hem of my coat sleeve. I didn't plan on telling anyone that, but the words tumbled out of my mouth before I could stop them. I feel like I've been through an emotional shredder and from the way Mel is looking at me, it must be visible on my face. "He offered to pay me so I could stop working for Black."

One of Mel's dark brows rises as her mouth opens. For a moment, she's speechless, which is super-weird. "What? What are you talking about?"

"He said he loves me, and offered to make me his mistress."

Mel blinks at me. "What'd you say?"

"I said no, that it wasn't my dream to be someone's mistress. I want more, and he doesn't—so Sean walked away." My voice is too soft, too steady. I blink away the stinging that's been building behind my eyes and smile at her. "I know you hated him, but he meant something to me. I just need to make sure I have no extra time so I can't think about him. I'll fill up my weekends with work and focus on school. It'll be all right."

"Honey, I don't know if you should—"

I start to walk past her with a plastic smile on my face. It feels so wrong, so utterly out of place. "I'm fine, Mel. I'll see you tonight. We can have pancakes for dinner. I know you've been dying to go to IHOP for a while."

Mel says she'll talk to me later, but she has that concerned look on her face—the kind people give when they know you're in over your head. I head down to my car and turn the engine over. I love that it starts on the first try. I love that the windows close and the seatbelt works. I stop thinking about these things because they lead my thoughts back to Sean.

CHAPTER 4

Captree is a little park down by Robert Moses beach. There are docks and that's where I go after stopping at a deli to grab an egg on a roll and a cup of coffee. I walk to the end of a pier, past some people waiting to board a fishing boat, sit down, and dangle my legs over the edge. It's not as cold today.

The wind whips my hair into my mouth as I bite down. I spit out the bite of sandwich and the hair and continue to claw at my tongue. I think I swallowed some hair, which skeeves me out.

"Hey, stranger," he says. I glance over my shoulder and see Marty standing behind me with his hands in the pockets of his corduroy barn coat. His hair is blown every which way, and his cheeks are rosy, like he's been down here for a while.

"What are you doing here?" I never figured out what to say to Marty after he told me that he had feelings for me. Besides, how do you forgive someone for lying like that?

You forgave Mel, my inner voice reminds me.

"I'm going out on a flounder boat for the day. Thought I'd do something manly for a change." He gives me a crooked smile.

My eyes don't meet his for long. I can't look at him without regret pooling into my mouth like vomit. I miss him, I know I do, but I don't know how to get past what he did. Do I just pretend it never happened? Do I act like Marty's just a friend, even when I know he wants more? Everything seems so hard and I wish to God that it wasn't. I want my Marty back, but that guy doesn't exist. This one does—the guy in the thick coat with the chapped cheeks.

"You know how to fish?"

"Not really," Marty steps closer and sits next to me. "How hard can it be?"

"You know you have to touch worms and shove hooks through their wriggling bodies, right?"

"Yup, I brought gloves." He pulls out a pair of yellow plastic dishwashing gloves, which makes me laugh.

"You can't use those!"

Marty gives me a sideways look that says he's teasing, trying to make me smile like he used to. It's weird how much a person can communicate with a single look. "I planned on wearing a yellow rain coat and matching boots, but I thought the other wharf guys would make fun of me."

"Ya think?"

"Yeah, but what's life without a little color?"

"You can drop the gay thing, Marty."

"What gay thing? A guy can't like yellow?" He bumps his shoulder into mine and I bump him back. I take a few bites of my sandwich before he says, "Are we good?"

I nod slowly. "Yeah, we're good, or close enough. Gooder, maybe."

The tension in Marty's shoulders lessens. I rip off a piece of my roll and hand it to him. Marty pops it into his mouth. "Would you like to come with me? I'm pretty sure the boat isn't full."

"Can't. I have to work this afternoon."

"Oh." Marty goes silent. It's like I took an ax to the conversation and killed it.

"Want to come to dinner with me and Mel later? We're IHOP-ing it."

"Yeah, sounds great. I'll have worked up a manly appetite by then, and will have a serious craving for some crepes." I laugh again and hand him another piece of my roll. Marty pops it into his mouth and says, "Don't hang out here by yourself for too long."

"Because of the bodies in the marsh? Marty that was a long time ago. No one is going to kill me."

"No, because I don't want the ghosts of the dead hookers to show up and give you tips."

I smack his shoulder hard and Marty fakes falling to the side. I grab his arm and pull him back before he really falls off the dock. I punch his arm lightly. It had been a teasing gesture between us once. I wonder if we'll ever have that back. The corner of my mouth tips up and I shake my head, laughing lightly. "Asshole."

"I told you I'm not gay. You can call me *dick*, now." He says it proudly, like *I'm a dick* should be plastered on his tee shirt.

"Go catch your boat, dick. They're going to leave without you." I shake my head as Marty jumps up. He looks down the dock to where his boat is boarding. A large scruffy man hollers last call.

"See you later?"

"Yeah."

When did my life turn to shit? Was it before or after I met Black? I'm not sure anymore. It seems that I traded one set of problems for another.

As I watch Marty board his boat, regret squeezes my ribcage with its giant hands. I wish things could go back to the way they were. Life before Black was less complicated. I was poor, but I had friends.

Now I have the cash I need to do what I want, but I've damaged all of my relationships—and my heart.

CHAPTER 5

When I get back to the room, Amber is gone. Relieved, I jump in the shower and let the scalding water turn me lobster-colored. When I get out, I step from the tiny bathroom with a towel around my body and dripping hair. I seriously need to do wash, because there never seem to be enough towels.

My phone chirps, so I walk over to it. Tucking a damp piece of hair behind my ear, I look down at the text message, hoping beyond reason that it's Sean and that he's changed his mind. But when I lift it and look at the screen, it isn't. Hope is stupid. It keeps making me do irrational things. Sean isn't coming back for me—he's gone. I need to accept it and move on.

There's a picture of Marty holding a tiny fish with his yellow gloves. It makes me smile. He's such a dork, but I know he sent it to try and cheer me up.

Mel plows through the door, and looks up at me. "Where the hell do you think we live? In fucking Banjo-land? Lock your damn door, Avery. I could have been a serial killer for Chrissakes."

"Or Naked Guy." Mel and I shudder in unison as our faces scrunch up in disgust. I grab my brush and start on my hair. "He offered to do me after Amber this morning. Real classy."

"You want me to show him my mad ninja skills with knives? That'll turn him whiter than he already is." Mel grins like she's thinking about something specific, which is a little bit scary.

"You don't need to cut anyone for me. I'm good." I flip my hair over and brush it out. "I'll take a rain check."

"Oh? You got plans or something?"

Flipping my hair back, I nearly fall over. Mel laughs at me as I blink and steady myself. "Nah, it's just Black. She kind of scares the crap out of me."

Mel makes a sound of agreement and plops down on my bed. It's still made and looked pretty before Mel rolled on it. She kicks off her shoes and pulls her feet up. "So, I guess now that Psycho Romeo is gone, you want out? All that talk this morning was just talk, right?"

"I can't quit. I need enough money to finish grad school." Mel doesn't say anything, but her expression speaks for her. She thinks that I should leave. "I'm going to load up my schedule now, sign a bunch of contracts, and then bust my ass in summer sessions. I have to prove to the university that I can handle the graduate work."

"How many contracts are you going to sign? I never sign more than one at a time. It seems too risky and Black isn't someone you mess around with, Avery. That's a seriously bad plan."

I feel dead inside, and it comes across in my voice when I speak. "I just want to get on with my life."

"So do I, but this is a seriously bad plan. Did you tell anyone else?"

My eyes flick up and meet hers. "You mean Marty? Not really. He said it was killing him. I don't want to hurt him."

"He'd tell you that you were being stupid. What would you tell him?"

"That I have to stay alive and this is the only way I know to do it."

Mel shakes her head. "You're making a mistake."

I'm so stressed out that I can't stand to hear her words right now. "I could really use your support on this. It's going to be hard enough without you telling me that I'm an idiot."

"Fine, let's talk. You have a client in a couple of hours. How are you going to do him? Black will start micromanaging you and ask this shit, so spit it out, Avery." My face flames red as my eyes dart away from hers. "Shit, girl. You still blush? How could you blush? You fucked Freak Show how many times now, and you still turn cherry red when someone mentions sex. How old are you? Twelve?"

I want to prove to her that I can handle this. I make up a bunch of stuff and say it looking her in the eye. I give enough details that her mouth opens slightly. "I'm not an idiot, I just don't like talking about it."

"Well, if you do that with Henry Thomas, Black will never ask you anything again."

I nod. "That's what I was thinking."

"Where'd you learn that shit from anyway? I didn't think you had it in you." Mel is halfway stuck between impressed and concerned. The only reason she's concerned is because it's me and I'm fragile.

But I'm sick of it. I wanted control over my life, so I took it. I learned what I need to know to do this job and I'll do it. "I looked it up. There was a Q&A from some chick that works a Vegas brothel. She posted it and a ton of guys said she was right—that it's majorly awesome. I figured that I have to be beyond acceptable to get Black off my back." I shrug like it doesn't matter.

Mel pushes off the bed. "I'm sorry I took you to Black. I screwed up, Avery. And that's the last I'm going to say about that, because no matter what we do, we can't change that. Not now. So, I'll help you out and be Ms. Supportive, no matter what crazy crap you decide."

CHAPTER 6

Gabe meets me at the elevators. Since it's Sunday afternoon the offices are empty. "What kind of company is here during the day?"

Gabe gives me a look that says I shouldn't be asking, but he answers anyway. "Calling center."

"For what? Insurance?"

He grins. "You could call it that."

Okay, so it's not an insurance center. My next guess is something tawdry like a phone sex operator calling center. Do they even have those? As I walk past desks, I imagine what it would have to sound like in here if that were going on, which doesn't match what I saw last time I walked in when everyone was working.

"She's not in a good mood, so don't piss her off. Say yes to whatever she offers and get the hell out." Gabe talks softly—well, for Gabe—and deposits me at Black's door. "I'll bring the car around and wait for you downstairs."

Gabe disappears and my heart races harder. I knock on the door, lightly.

Miss Black snaps, "Enter." When I push into the room, I see her sorting through papers, looking beyond irritated. There's a ruler clutched in her right hand and a pen in the other. "I see you lost another client."

"Who was the first one?"

Miss Black stops what she's doing and looks up at me sharply. She drops the pen and snaps her fingers at me. "Take it off. I have no time for you right now." She snaps again before I realize she wants me to disrobe.

I wriggle out of my black dress and stand there like livestock. At least I'm not naked. Miss Black circles me with her hand on her chin and that ruler gripped loosely in her hand. I'm wearing a lacy black shelf bra that doesn't contain my nipples. It's paired with a garter belt that's holding up lace-topped thigh highs and a panty that's nothing more than a piece of string.

I seriously hate this part of inspection. As Miss Black passes behind me, I'm whacked on my backside. I yelp and feel the sting of the ruler. I round on her. Before I can say anything, she shakes her head, like she's upset with me. "You're not taking care of yourself, Avery. Your backside is too wide."

"It is not! I weigh the same as I did when I got here."

"You had more muscle when you got here. Firm that up immediately. Our girls don't have droopy cheeks."

I glance down at my ass. It's not droopy. I want to argue with her, but I don't. Gabe's warning is in my mind, so I nod and agree with her. "I'll fix it."

"You will or I'll fix it for you, set you up with some men who will firm it up due to their particular preferences, if you catch my meaning."

I nod. "Whatever you think, Miss Black." I despise this part. I wish it was over, but Black stands there with her ruler like she wants to beat me with it.

She snaps at me. "Get dressed. I'm tired of looking at you."

As I pull on my dress, I ask, "Do you have more work for me?"

Miss Black looks at me and laughs, like I'm asking for something crazy. "You want more work? You haven't had sex with two clients yet and you're asking for more?"

I nod as I zip up my dress. "I'll take care of Mr. Thomas."

"You will or I'll give you to one of the mindless security thugs as a plaything." Miss Black is shifting through papers on her desk as she speaks. "Since you're so determined, here is a new client. I don't have his papers completed yet and I'm still waiting on pictures, but he wanted to book you for next weekend."

"Me? He specifically asked for me?"

"Yes, although I don't see why." She shoves a blank contract at me. "Sign this and I'll get the rest filled in later." I take the pen and sign. She shoves a preferences sheet at me. "Update this as well."

I flip the paper around and look up at her. "I get paid more if it's blank, right?" She nods. Her dark eyes hold mine for a moment, like she thinks I'm weak. It pisses me off. I'm not weak. I've put up with more crap than she has, I'm sure of it. Besides, after what Sean did to me, I don't see how anything could be worse. I push the paper back to her, blank.

"Do you expect me to be impressed? You play these games, Avery, but can you honestly perform when a client wants to have anal sex with you? What if he wants to use beads? Clamps? Or other things that frighten you? You're all talk, and I know it. Check off the things you won't do on the sheet."

Shaking my head, I say, "No, I'm in this up to my neck. I don't care what he wants to do, I'll do it."

"This client specifically requested some odd things. Last chance, little girl. Don't bite off more than you can chew, because he will demand it, and have every right to take it from you." It feels like she's trying to scare me off, but I don't let her.

I fold my arms over my chest. "Can I go now?"

She grins triumphantly and I realize that I was played. Her tactics are making me keep that sheet blank. "Yes, dear. Go and make sure Mr. Thomas comes begging for more."

CHAPTER 7

My stomach is twisting in knots as Gabe drives me closer to the hotel. I fish my bracelet out of my bag and put it on. My hand is shaking so much that I have trouble getting the clasp to lock. When Gabe hits a pothole, I fumble and drop it.

"Sorry about that. The streets haven't been the same since Sandy." They really haven't. That damn hurricane literally ate half the seashore, along with Ocean Parkway and a ton of houses. There are parts of Long Island that look abandoned with houses that look like skeleton's covered in black mold. Tattered tarps have been shredded to ruins like the building beneath.

"It's okay. I'm just nervous, I guess."

Gabe is uncharacteristically silent. It drives me nuts, so I blurt out, "Just say it. Yell at me for not wearing a coat and agreeing to sleep with half of New York. Go ahead and say it. It won't make any difference now anyway."

"Which is why I'm not saying nothing." Gabe's old eyes meet mine in the rearview mirror. The car dips again as it moves over uneven pavement. A car cuts off someone in front of us and horns blare before the telltale sound of a collision.

"Awh, Jesus Christ—" Gabe lurches the car to the side while I try to get my bracelet around my wrist. It catches just as the old guy takes a less conventional route around the accident with two tires up on the sidewalk. He leans on his horn and the pedestrians jump out of the way.

I glance behind us to see a wake of angry people flipping us the bird with extra enthusiasm. I hold onto my 'oh shit' strap and try not to scream. Gabe goes down half a city block on the curb before getting around the accident. "Sorry, if we're late, Black will skin me. She's in a foul mood."

"Why? She doesn't have enough money to roll around in?" My arms are folded over my chest. I repress a shiver but it makes me spasm anyway.

Gabe reaches over and cranks up the heater. "Nah, supply and demand problems. She has more client requests than she can fill. Black knows she's losing money and pissing away cash ticks her off."

"What?" This is news to me. I thought I was expendable, as in totally replaceable. "Like she doesn't have enough call girls?"

Gabe smirks at me in the mirror. "I didn't say that. Did you hear me say that?"

Crazy old man. I shake my head and smile at him. "Just because you didn't say it doesn't mean anything. She'll kill you if she figures out that you told me anything."

"Yeah, but I'm the one she sends for shit like that and it's not like I plan on roughing up my own face, so I think we're okay.

"Besides, my point is that she needs you. Don't let her push you into things you don't want to do. You're a tenderfoot with all this. You shouldn't have more than one guy a weekend—she knows that—but she accepted these clients and has to deliver someone."

"So she's sending me? What about all that stuff about preferences and trying to set us up with guys that are my type?"

Gabe snorts. "Princess, right now, every guy is your type."

This doesn't sit right with me. I glance out the window and wonder if she played me. All those times that Black tried to get me to sign the preference sheet and I didn't—I wonder if she manipulated me. Am I that stupid?

Maybe.

Mel's words ring in my ears, *It's fun, like a really good date.* But it isn't. I feel like I'm being bought and sold. I don't feel powerful or sexy when I do this. No, it just feels like I've lost control of my life, that I have to do these things to survive.

Resentment is lodged in the back of my throat. I swallow it down because it won't do me any good now. I have to cram my emotions into a box and lock them up, or I'll cry. I can't even imagine what Black would do with that.

Gabe stops in front of the hotel. Before he opens the door, he shoots me a look. "I'm keeping a close proximity tonight for obvious reasons. Black wants confirmation the deed is done." The corners of his eyes are wrinkled, like he's seen too many sunrises that made his gaze narrow with disgust. The guy is a fighter and for some reason he's looking out for me.

I nod and slip out of the car when the hotel person opens my door. It's a young guy, maybe a year or two younger than me. His dark eyes sweep over me once and he smiles. "Good afternoon, Miss."

If this guy complimented me like that a few weeks ago with his flirty smile, I would have felt something, but now I just nod. There's no normalcy any longer. The young man looks taken down a notch, although I didn't mean to do it. It's like the other night when I was talking to Sidney—Peter's girlfriend. I said something stupid and accidentally insulted her. In my head it sounded light and playful but when it fell out of my mouth, well, I know I was a bitch for saying it. I wasn't myself that night. I haven't been myself for a long time. What happens to people when they lose sight of who they are? Can they ever come back? Is the old version of me gone forever, or can I pull her back from the depths?

Since my parents died, my life has been filled with nightmares, and grief so thick it feels like globs of fat, coating my skin, suffocating me day by day. The fake smile that spreads across my lips as I smooth my silk dress, the slight sashay to my walk, the confidence in my stance, it's all fake. A few male heads turn as I walk by. I know this by now. Something about a confident, well dressed woman makes them look. They wonder who I am and where I'm going, and a good chunk of those guys wonder how it would be to get between my legs. They admire the man who landed me. I've seen many impressed glances the times I was with Sean or Henry in public. But the truth is, if anyone dared to look, they'd notice that I have no idea what I'm doing and I don't care. Maybe if I act like I'm into whatever

Henry wants, then he won't notice that I'd rather be anywhere but here.

If I could only be so lucky.

As I walk through the front doors to the hotel, I confidently move toward the elevators. This is the same place I met Henry the last time I tried this. My stomach is twisting in knots as beads of sweat break out across my forehead. The elevator doors shimmer as they open and I step inside. I dab away the perspiration on my face, terrified that I'm going to hurl in the elevator before I even make it to his door, but I'm not stopping. I won't quit—not that I have the option—and it's not like Henry is horrible. He's actually pretty sweet, but I don't feel like that toward him, and that's the problem. I don't feel anything toward Henry, except friendship.

That's why I'm turning into a plastic person. You know, the kind who are so fake they've forgotten how to be real. If it helped me forget the pain shooting through my heart every time it beat, I'd sign on the line and never look back.

The nausea makes my stomach lurch. I open my purse and dig out an alcohol wet wipe. After tearing the top open, I inhale deeply and the over-salivating thing stops. When I was in fourth grade, I had horrible nerves like this and the nurse had me sniff a cotton ball with some rubbing alcohol on it. Apparently, the smell can short circuit the part of the brain that's pressing the vomit button like a chimp jacked up on Pixie Stix.

I have to hold it together. When the elevator doors open, I manage a smile. My mind keeps replaying the scenes from the last time I saw Henry, which isn't helping me any. This time the act has to be thicker and the lies falling off my lips have to be so deep that they become real.

Stepping out, I manage to smile and walk down the hall to his room. *This is it, Stanz. Jump in or run like hell and hope Gabe doesn't bother to hunt you down.* Before I can lift my hand to knock, the door flies open. Henry is standing on the other side with an ice bucket in his hand. He startles and nearly jumps out of his skin.

"Avery, I didn't hear you knock. Please come in, make yourself comfortable while I grab some ice." He holds the door for me. I smile at him and duck under his arm and into the room. "Be right back, love."

"All right." I walk into the little room. It's just a bed and bathroom, like last time. I wish I loved getting wasted because I'd be so schnockered right now. I put my purse down and walk over to the window and look out at the city. The sky is inky blue with a smearing of fluffy clouds that are hard to see because of the tall buildings.

The door opens and Henry pockets his key card. He's wearing a cream button down shirt that's open at the neck along with a pair of gray slacks. His hair is a little less perfect than usual, like something's been stressing him out and he ran his fingers through it a million times.

"I hope you don't mind, but I took the liberty of ordering champagne. I actually have some exciting news, which is why I really wanted to see you this weekend." Henry puts the ice bucket down and crosses the room. On the desk there is a bottle of champagne already chilled. He lifts it out and takes up a glass flute like he's done this a thousand times before.

I step toward him. This is going to make it much harder to not get shitfaced. I failed to eat before coming so this will go straight to my head, and as it is I'm a lightweight when it comes to drinking. Still, I smile at him as I walk over and I place my hands on his shoulders as he tops off my glass. Henry turns, grinning at me, and hands me the bubbling liquid. "So, what's the exciting news?"

"My design worked. You know how I wanted Ferro's patent?" I nod and sip. "Well, everyone was telling me that what I wanted to do couldn't be done, but it worked. The prototype was completed Friday morning and it worked!"

"That's great, Henry! What is it? What does it do?" I tuck a piece of hair behind my ear and take another sip.

My mind wanders; I think I can outrun Gabe on foot. I could dart out the door and vanish. No one would ever see me again. I have enough money to live in a shack in some little town off the grid. I could do it— but I'd hate it. More thoughts flash into my head and disappear just as quickly, but no matter what, there is no way out of this.

"I don't think you'd understand. It's complicated." Henry watches me sip. For some reason his words feel like an insult.

I twirl the stem of the glass between my fingers and look up at him. "I'm smart. Try me."

"Very well, but first tell me who was keeping you from me yesterday and the day before? As soon as I found out the good news about my invention, I wanted to celebrate—and I wanted to do it with you—however your employer wouldn't arrange it. So," Henry slips his hands around my waist and pulls me to him so that our hips bump. His grip is firm, possessive. "Tell me who I'm playing second fiddle to this weekend."

I laugh lightly, like he's funny. "Henry, you know there's no one else that I'd rather be with—"

"So Black was just creating supply issues to make me crave you more? Because I already crave you more than is reasonably healthy."

"Cravings can be good…" I throw back the rest of the contents in my glass and set it down.

Henry's gaze follows my movements. He tips his head to the side and whispers. "What are you craving, love?" Henry leans in and presses his lips to mine. He kisses me and I force myself to kiss him back, even though I don't want to. When he pulls away, there's a sparkle in his eye, like he knows something that I don't.

"What's that look?" I ask.

"You're too sweet to me, always trying to protect my feelings, but I know who you were with this weekend. I saw you two together." The floor of my stomach drops like someone cut the elevator cord. Before I can say anything, Henry stops me. "I knew you had other clients, but I didn't imagine you were screwing him." The idea of me fucking Sean obviously upset him.

I touch Henry's arm lightly and look into his eyes. "Then don't. Tonight there is no one else, it's just you and me."

He shakes his head. "It'll never be just you and me. I should probably stow it and just shag you until I'm satisfied, but I can't stand the idea of you being with him. Do you know who he is? What he's done?"

Things are spinning out of control. My pulse pounds faster, so that it's banging in my head like a drum. "I don't really get a say in things, Henry. And I'm here with you now. I can celebrate with you now." I try to touch him, but his hand flies out and he swats me away. The action surprises me and I don't know what to say.

Henry's voice sounds light, like it doesn't matter, but it clearly does. "Yeah? And how should I take you? I'd rather not share the same woman with Ferro, but if I have to, tell me where he fucked you so I don't get his leftovers."

This isn't like him. "Henry? What's going on? You *hired* me. Did you really think you were the only client I had?"

"I wanted you to myself."

"It doesn't work that way."

Henry grabs my wrist hard and yanks me toward him. When Sean did things like that it felt exciting, but right now warning bells are going off in my head. Something isn't right, but I think I'm overreacting.

Henry's jaw is clenched tight and his eyes narrow to thin slits. He hisses in my face, "Maybe it should."

"You're hurting me." I try to twist away from him, but I can't. My pulse freaks out. This is wrong. Something has broken in this guy's brain—I see it in his eyes. Every instinct I have is telling me to haul ass out of there, but the guy has a lobster-like hold on me and he's fucking twisting. I bend my arm so that my wrist doesn't snap and yell, "Henry, let go!"

But he doesn't release me. Instead, he gets up in my face. When he speaks, his breath washes over my face. I expect him to say something, like he's hurting me on purpose, but he doesn't. "You have to know what you did to me, how I felt when I called with good news and couldn't see you for two days.

"So, I waited, and the entire time I thought about you—and what he was doing to you—and how you let him. That's unacceptable, and I intend to show you exactly what I mean, love. You're mine." It's like he's possessed. He continues to twist my wrist so hard that the skin burns, forcing it up behind my back. He holds it there, driving me onto my knees.

I'm close to hysterically screaming. It's climbing up my throat, accompanied by raw terror. Black didn't seem to screen this guy for crazy, because Henry has bat-shit crazy coming out of his ears.

Mind racing, I decide to go with what he wanted in the first place—me. Henry wanted me to be his girlfriend. He took this arrangement instead, because it was the only way to get me. Now, I see that he's not the charming guy I thought he was. Sean is devious, wicked, and maybe even evil, but this guy is insane.

And that's the thing that scares me the most—crazy people are irrational—they do things that don't make sense, and right now Henry is close to breaking my wrist. He doesn't seem to realize that what he's doing is bringing tears to my eyes and a tremor to my already strained voice. I try to talk him down, to bring him back enough to grab my bracelet and smash the black bead. All I have to do is get him to let go for a second.

Steadying my voice, I say, "I'm here now, Henry. I want to hear about everything. We can do anything you want—

anything at all. Just let go of my hand and I'm all yours."

His eyes blaze with fury. Holy fuck did I say the wrong thing. "No! You're not! You were with him!" Henry makes a strangled sound in the back of his throat. He releases my wrist and throws me to the floor. "Do you know? Do you even know! That fucker ruined my life! He took her away and now he's done it again! Because there is no way in hell that I am going to let that son of a bitch do it again!"

Henry continues to bellow at me. I have no idea what he's talking about, but there's a river of bad blood between Henry and Sean. Holy shit, it's like a deluge of hatred. His eyes aren't even focused anymore. Henry looks as nuts as he sounds. He's ranting, with his hands flying, screaming at me like I planned to do this to him.

I never wanted to hurt him, but right now I'm so scared that he's going to kick me and smash my ribs. I roll onto my side as he screams, then gracelessly crab-crawl away from him, and finally take a second to jump to my feet. Reaching for my wrist, I feel for the bracelet. Taking my eyes off of

Henry would be beyond stupid right now, but my palm only grabs flesh. Frantically, I feel for the black bead, but it's not there. I chance it and look down.

Horror washes over me when I stare at my wrist. The bracelet is gone. It's not there. My pulse pounds in my ears, drowning out everything the crazy man is saying. Henry's ticking things off on his fingers and stepping toward me, like I personally fucked up his life. As I scan the floor of the room for the bracelet, his words finally sink in.

"Are you even listening to me, you fucking whore!" Just as I look up, his palm collides with the side of my face. Pain explodes in my cheek as my face whips sideways. Henry grabs me by the shoulders and pins my arms to my sides.

His voice gets freaky calm. The death grip he has on my shoulders loosens and he pets my arms like I'm a cat. "This is your fault, you know. I normally don't get this bent out of shape over the little things." As if fucking Sean was a little thing. How many times has this guy been cheated on? Is that why he's freaking out? "Today could have been perfect. God knows how hard I tried, love. I tried to put it behind me, to forgive you, but once you walked in here with that slutty dress and that beautiful smile, I kept looking at your mouth. I thought about shoving my cock in between those hot lips and enjoying you like I should. I deserve a good time after what I've been through, I do. And you were supposed to be it, but then I kept thinking about it and looking at those lips, and those tits in that dress—and it just kills me that he had you first." Henry takes a breath and tries to steady himself.

"I'm a forgiving man, I am. Just ask any of my exes and they'll tell you that I don't hold a grudge under normal circumstances, but bloody hell—this is so far beyond normal that I can't handle it. I can't…" By the time he's done talking, his voice is so high and airy that I'm seriously considering jumping out the window. I can't get past him to run out the door. What floor are we on? I'm pretty sure a three to four story jump will break my legs and I'm up higher than that.

I'm talking. I don't know what I'm saying, but my voice is soothing, soft. My palms are up towards him like he's going to hurt me and I'm begging him to stop. "You can. You can handle anything, Henry. You can handle this."

Slowly, his eyes raise and he looks at me. A bolt of frigid fear shoots through my stomach and lodges in my gut. "Tell me something."

I nod. "Anything." My gaze flicks around the room for the bracelet, but it's gone. It's so gone. The clasp must have been broken. It's probably outside the building in a gutter. Gabe is going to find my chopped up body at Captree tomorrow if I don't figure out how to get out of here. I make my decision and wait for his question.

"How do you live with yourself? You see what you've done to me and I'm sure you've done it to other men. You're an addiction, and an anomaly. You have a wickedly sinful body, like you've used it to get what you wanted your whole life, but there's this wholesome, chaste thing about you—like you have no idea how to use that body—like you're shocked when some guy looks at you like he wants you. You can't be both. It's not possible to be a virgin slut, but somehow you are."

I have no idea how to answer that. My eyes dart between Henry and the door. He notices and the corner of his mouth tugs up. "Do you want to leave? I haven't even gotten what I paid for yet."

Yeah, there's no way in hell I'm having sex with him now. I don't do crazy. "I really think we should reschedule."

"Yeah?" He steps towards me and I step back. He grins like it's funny, like he knows that he's scaring me. "Why? Do you have another client after this? Or is it Ferro again?" Henry steps forward and I step back. He advances on me until my back hits the wall.

"I want what I paid for, skank." Henry places his hands on my shoulders and leans, forcing all his weight onto me. My knees buckle and I kneel between him and the wall. I don't wait for him to whip it out, I act. With all the force I can muster, I draw back my fist and slam it into his junk, while his hands are occupied by his zipper. Henry gasps and doubles over.

I jump out of the way before he can catch me, but I'm too close the wall. His hand grabs the back of my neck as I race past him. His other hand is there in a flash, strangling me. Rapidly, I step backward, trying to pry his fingers off my neck. I'm screaming at him, but my voice is being choked into silence.

My knees hit the back of the bed and he pushes me down. The crazed look in his eyes tells me that he's going to do more than fuck me. He has every intention of hurting me as much as he can. I can sense it even though he never says a word. The silence is thick, suffocating me. I watch in terror as Henry chokes me. A bead of sweat rolls down my temple. His eyes track it as his hands grab at my thighs and shoves my hem out of the way. The beautiful panty is ripped away. When Henry goes to crawl on top of me, something crunches on the floor under his foot. I hear it, but the sound doesn't register. My heartbeat is a million times louder.

Henry straddles me. His pants are still on, half undone, and his hands reach for my face. He leans in close, pinning me to the bed. Resting a hand on either side of my face, he strokes me over and over again— slow and creepy. The whites around his eyes are exposed as he stares at my neck without blinking. His hands drift there to the soft spot at the hollow of my throat. His thumb strokes the vulnerable place softly, like he knows that pressing into it will crush my windpipe.

I'm going to die. My death wish is finally coming true, and it's not until this moment that I realize how much I want to live. This can't be the end, it can't be. I worked too hard and came too damn far on my own to be killed by this man, but there's nothing I can do. I can't bite, kick, or claw my way out of this. It's not until that instant that the tears start cascading down my cheeks.

Henry closes his hand into a fist and positions his thumb on top of the soft skin on my neck, staring, like he's mesmerized. He savors the moment, slowly twisting his wrist and feeling me gasping for air as the pressure increases, bit by bit. Before Henry pushes all the way down and buries his thumb in my neck, the door is kicked open. Wood shards fly across the room as the doorjamb breaks apart. Henry looks up just in time to see Gabe coming at him. One of the old guy's beefy hands collides with Henry's side.

As Gabe lands the punch, he says, "Ride's over, asshole." Henry is launched off the bed and hits the floor like a rag doll. Gabe walks around and says, "This is from me, personally." Gabe's leg swings, and wheezing sounds of pain come from Henry.

Jumping off the bed, I run over and grab Gabe's arm before he can kick Henry again. "Don't," I plead and tug on his arm. "Just get me out of here. Please."

Gabe stops and turns back to look at me. "Gather your things, Miss Stanz, and meet me in the hallway. There are consequences for messing with Miss Black's girls. I need to make sure the message is received."

I'm shaking. I don't notice it until I try to nod and can't. Taking my purse, I turn my back on them both and walk out the door.

CHAPTER 8

"Avery, you all right?" Mel asks as she skewers a hotcake and pops it into her mouth. I couldn't manage to tell her what happened with Henry. I covered the slight black and blue on my cheek and smile a lot, hoping that she won't ask questions.

As it was, Black asked a million questions and wasn't convinced that it wasn't my fault until Gabe spoke. The only bright side to today was the huge check.

Apparently when a client tries to kill one of Black's girls, we get compensated.

The money is burning a hole in my pocket. I want to get rid of it, but I can't. I know that would be stupid, but it feels tainted. I nearly died earning that bit of cash.

"Yeah, you've been uncharacteristically quiet." Marty picks up a sausage and makes an obscene gesture.

Mel sneers at him. "Cut it out, dickwad. You don't have to pretend to be bi or homo or whatever the hell you were doing before. And I think Avery forgave you way too fast for pulling shit like that, so don't piss me off or I will stab you with my fork. Then, my pancakes will get bloody and I'll have to kill you with my spoon."

Marty blinks at her. The shock is short lived. He grins. "I bet you've done lots of things with a spoon." He winks at Mel and then stabs a sausage and hands it to her. "It's demonstration time."

Mel's amber eyes widen as her mouth falls open. "Holy shit. You did not just say that to me. Did he really just say that, Avery?"

I'm lost in thought, wondering about everything and nothing. My mind skips between things that seemed pointless at the time, but now mean something. If that light at Prairie Drive didn't take so damn long, I would have never met Sean. There are little things like that flooding my mind, and I can't stop them.

Mel bumps my shoulder. "Hello? What's with you? He told me to suck off a sausage in the middle of IHOP."

I shrug. "So, do it."

Marty tries to hide his laughter under a napkin as Mel gives me a WTF face. She blinks and a second later, she grabs the fork and is doing sexy things to the sausage. I'm leaning on my hand, staring blankly, but I'm aware enough to know Marty is transfixed by whatever Mel is doing—and so are the guys in the next booth. They'd been talking about some game way too loudly and now all three of them are silently watching Mel give her breakfast a blowjob.

I glance at her out of the corner of my eye, like I'm bored. "I wouldn't swallow that if I were you. I'm pretty sure it'll be all grease. You'll gain ten pounds in one gulp."

Mel nearly chokes and puts the thing on her plate. The three guys are now staring at me, as well. Mel starts laughing, but she has a strange smile on her face. "You're talking a bit too loud there, Avery."

"You're blowing your breakfast, Mel. I don't think it matters much." I glance up at her, after folding my napkin into a swan. My mom taught me how to fold napkins before she died. It was her last hobby.

One of the guys across from us stands and walks over to our table. He gives Marty the guy nod and says to me and Mel, "There are very few women who demand attention the way you do."

Mel laughs, "Which one of us are you talking to there, Slick?"

The guy smiles. He's attractive, with sandy blonde hair that's not too long or too short. Coupled with a firm body and blazing blue eyes, he's a hottie. "What makes you think I was only talking to one of you?" He leans forward and places his hands on the table. There's a silver ring at the base of his thumb. I stare at it for a second too long. He says to me, "Cock ring. Comes in handy, so I just carry it with me."

"It's kind of small." I flick my eyes up to his. I don't feel like fending him off right now. It was the quickest shortcut to getting rid of him.

He grins and looks at me. "There's nothing small about me, baby." Mel's eyes flick between me and the guy. She'd normally cut off his balls, but today she isn't.

"Prove it," Mel blurts out. "Whip that sucker out right now and show us the miraculous marvel that is tucked into those tight jeans." Mel sweeps her eyes to his waist and then dips her gaze lower. When the guy doesn't move, she glances up. "Well, come on. I don't have all day. Besides, me and my friend here will only do a three way if the guy has a really big dick."

The guy swallows hard. "A three way?"

"You walked over to the right table. In fact, my friend here is sometimes gay, so if you play your cards right, you might get a four way." Mel laugh-smirks as she inclines her head toward Marty, who, in turn, wiggles the tips of his fingers at the guy. "So, whip it out and show us. If it's big enough, we'll make your wettest dreams come true."

The guy stands there like he doesn't know what to do. His friends are laughing, egging him on. A waitress brushes past him and the guy nearly jumps out of his skin. "You're just shittin' with me." The guy smiles and turns to walk back to his table.

Mel shrugs. "Well, now you'll never know." When he looks back at her, Mel winks at him.

He laughs like she's kidding and slips into his booth. Their conversation continues in hushed whispers. They keep looking over at us.

"You're evil. You know that?" I say, and shake my head. "Let's get out of here before this turns into an urban legend."

Mel slips out of the booth. "Oooh! I like that! If you see a girl sucking off a sausage at the IHOP on Sunrise Highway, then you'll be invited to have a three way with her and her hot friend. Totally the stuff legends are made of. Damn, I love breakfast!" Mel glances at the table of guys and licks her finger seductively. Then, she points at the guy we were talking to. "Could have been you."

"You were joking. It wasn't a real offer." The guy is smiling, and it sounds like he's trying to convince himself. His friends are smiling hard, watching him.

Marty says, "That's what you think. Why do you think they let me hang out with them?" He mouths *huge dick* and waggles his eyebrows. As we walk out, the guy's friends start teasing him for passing up two hot chicks.

"Well, you totally screwed with that guy, and I helped make the legend of the Long Island sluts into a real thing. I bet it's floating around Facebook by morning." Marty walks next to me, smirking triumphantly. Mel is ahead of us, speed walking to the car.

I fold my arms across my chest and walk. There hasn't been much of a smile on my face tonight and Marty knows me too well. "So, what happened?"

My eyes cut to the side. "What are you talking about?"

"At work, something happened. What was it? You seem spooked." He touches my

H.M. WARD

forearm lightly, stopping me. We're standing in the middle of the parking lot. I look up at him, wanting to tell him, but afraid of what he'll say. "Just tell me. I think I already know. The asshole messed with you, right?"

"How'd you know that?"

"It's all over your face. Are you okay? Do I need to break his neck?"

I shake my head. "No, Gabe took care of him and got me out before he really had a chance to hurt me. Somehow his crazy got past Black. She didn't know he was jealous or nuts."

"Jealous? Who would order a call girl and then be jealous?"

"A crazy person. He hates Sean and when he realized I was with Sean this weekend, he went nuts. He would have killed me if Gabe didn't show up. I'm kind of out of it, that's all." I start walking again. Mel has started the car. The sky is that dingy gray, like it's going to snow again.

"Hey, wait." He takes my elbow and I stop and turn back to him. "Are you serious? The guy really wanted to hurt you?" I nod. Marty gives me the most grieved look I've seen on him yet. I know what he wants to say, but he swallows it back down. "I'm glad you're all right—I wish to God you'd quit—but I'm so glad you're all right." He pulls me into a hug and releases me before I can protest.

"I can't quit, Marty. You know that." My head hangs forward as we walk the rest of the way to Mel's car.

"When do you work again?"

"Next weekend, I guess. My regulars left, or had Gabe beat the shit out of them, so I guess I'll have a new guy next week. Black will clue me in closer to the weekend. In the meantime, I need to get caught up on school."

Marty nods solemnly, like he knows that he can't save me. I wish he could. I wish someone could pull me back, but I've already fallen into the abyss. Last time Sean was there to keep me company, but now I'm completely alone.

CHAPTER 9

By the time Wednesday night rolls around, I can't think. My mind keeps floating back to Sean. I hate that he left, but at the same time, I realize that I let him walk away. I didn't have to do that. I could have done something, some huge gesture, that swept him off his feet, but I didn't. I walked away and so did he.

I push my economics book away and wonder what the hell I was thinking when I chose my electives this semester. It's not my thing. I have to study twice as hard to keep up, so I invoked my failsafe plan to ensure my A- at the end of the semester—smile. It sounds really stupid, but before my freshman year I never smiled unless I felt like it. I'm not a smiley person, I guess.

Anyway, I had a sociology class and learned that people have a hard time thinking poorly of a person if that person is always smiling at them. Short version—I smile at the economics professor during the entire lecture. It doesn't matter if I'm bored out of my mind, or if I understand a thing he's said. I look pleased as punch to be there and maintain light eye contact. Oddly, I thought that would make him call on me more often, but it doesn't. He thinks I'm enthralled and paying attention, so unless I raise my hand, the prof calls on some other kid that's just as lost as I am. That little smile has pulled my average up a letter grade, because I have no interest in any of this.

I should have taken a sociology elective. Then, I could have glared at the teacher the whole time and sulked in peace rather than faking it the whole semester.

I tap the cover of the textbook with my pen and decide that I need to get out of here for a while and go back to the last place I was happy. I jump in the shower before Amber and the male slut return, and I get dressed. Around the time I'm almost ready, Mel knocks on my door and sticks her head inside before I answer.

"Avery, you here?" Mel catches a glimpse of me in my little black dress—the one that was mine before I started working for Miss Black. Mel steps into the room and folds her arms over her chest, knowing damn well that I don't have a client. "Tell me that you aren't going on a date."

I'm swiping on mascara and almost poke my eye out with the wand. I glance over at her from the other side of the room. "Nah, nothing like that. I just need to go out, get some fresh air. No guys."

"What about girls?"

I smirk and think of Sidney. "I don't do girls. Although I think Marty liked the idea of me and you together."

Mel plops down on my bed and smirks. "Every guy likes the idea of two girls together." She leans back on her elbows, careful not to mess up the bedspread. "So, I hear things, ya know. Things that I should have heard from you." I glance up at her in the mirror, wondering where this is going. "Are you going to tell me or do I have to keep up the twenty questions?"

"Depends on what you're asking about."

"Well, aren't you all evasive today? Okay, girlfriend, if you want to play that way I'm just gonna come out and say it—Gabe beat the shit out of your client the other night. I heard Black talking to him about it when I checked in earlier. She said you smashed the bead. What the hell happened? I thought that guy was sweetness in a pasty Brittish wrapper."

"So did I, until he went nuts. Apparently, he and Sean go way back. Let's just say that Henry has some serious anger issues. I don't want to talk about it." I finish applying my make-up and sweep a light dusting of blush over my cheeks. I look better, but I still feel like crap.

"I get it, but you should tell me this shit. I want to know if Black is accepting guys that she shouldn't. I haven't had to use that ugly little bracelet. Good to know it works, right?"

"Yeah," I say, and lean back on my dresser. "I can't imagine what would happen if the bead broke by accident. Gabe would pound the guy and ask questions later."

"Probably so, but hey, that's not my problem as long as he doesn't try to beat the shit out of me."

I'm watching her and too many questions rush through my mind. How is she okay living like this? How many times has she booked a client and had it go poorly? Maybe I'm just the worst hooker ever. I don't know, but I want to talk to her. At the same time, I'm guessing she'll flip out when I tell her where I'm going. Screw it. It's worth her freak out to have her along. "Come with me."

"Where are we going?"

"To the Crystal Lounge in the city."

"Isn't that where—"

"Yeah, it is." I cut her off before she can say more. "I'm heading to the bar for a while and I'd like company if you want to come."

She gives me a sad smile, like I'm pathetic. "He won't be there, Avery."

"I know Sean won't be there. That isn't why I'm going. It's hard to explain, but it's easier for me to move forward when I go back to the last place where I was happy and it was there. I was laughing the other night. Maybe it's stupid, but I'm all for whatever works and I need a mood shift. So, are you coming or not?"

"Psh, and pass up an invite to a swank bar? I don't think so. Give me a couple of minutes to get ready."

Mel is dressed and back in my room quickly. She's wearing a skin tight, ruched red dress that shows off every ample curve. Mel tosses her shoes on my bed as she fastens on a pair of huge gold earrings.

"How are you going to walk from the station to the hotel in those?"

"Who says we're walking anywhere?"

"I didn't want to take a cab."

"Nope, no cab. We're riding in style. Limo, baby." I raise an eyebrow at her. Although Mel has money, she rarely spends it. Wasting a bunch of hard-earned cash on a ride isn't like her. She waves me off. "I got connections—well, actually a guy owes me a favor, so I called it in. He'll be here in ten. Then, I can wear these babies and look every inch of luscious I want."

I smirk at her. After she straps her heels on her feet, we walk down the stairwell and wait for the limo. Mel points to the car when the headlights are in view and pushes through the door. Neither of us bothers with a wrap. Wraps are for losers. We duck into the car and when I look up, I'm shocked to see a familiar face.

"Gabe?" I ask, as I look between him and Mel.

"I'm sorry, but you must have me confused with someone else. My name is Gabriel and I don't work for Black and take her limos out when no one is looking." He looks up in the rear view mirror and smirks.

"She's going to kill you!"

Mel shakes her head. "Avery, stop fussing. He's just messing with you. Black gave him the car to get it cleaned up for some hotshot client this weekend. He's going to drop us off and then take the car in. Black won't even know we were in it."

"I thought you said a guy owed you a favor?" I ask, narrowing my gaze at her with a light smile on my lips. Mel has a way of making everything work to her advantage. I wish I knew how to do that.

"He does. I took his nephew to a wedding a couple of weeks ago and kept the dumb kid from knocking up his ex." Mel leans forward in the seat and says to Gabe, "By the way, that chick was insane."

"He bought you for his nephew?" I'm blinking at her, wondering what the hell she did.

Gabe answers for her. "You think I got no class? I don't buy my nephews hookers, damn, Avery. And like I'd mix business and pleasure that way. Nah, Mel watched out for him—he just didn't know it. He thinks he picked her up in a bar on the way there. I provided the ride—"

"And I happened to be at the bar, dressed to attend a wedding, and on the lookout for Gabe's hot nephew. And he is hot, just a little too heartbroken to see that the love of his life is a total bitch."

Mel and Gabe chatter, which is weird. They didn't get along at all when I first met him, and now it seems like they're old friends. Either way, it works for me.

"Where to, Miss Stanz?" When I tell him, he breaks our gaze and shakes his head softly, like he shouldn't say anything. "You sure about that?"

"Yeah, she's sure about that. Drive man! Stop asking us questions." Mel laughs and leans back into the seat. She starts chattering about tabloid gossip and I love her for it. "Did you see that shot of Trystan Scott?"

"Yeah, I did. When rockers come to town, they rock hard, huh?"

"I don't know. The guy seems…"

"Unlucky. Very unlucky." That guy's life has been plastered across the papers ever since they found him hiding in a high school on Long Island. He wrote a love song for some girl that didn't know he was alive. The song went viral, but the guy wouldn't show his face. Some blonde outed him. I feel bad for him. His life sucked and fame doesn't seem to have made it better.

"Cursed is more like it," Mel says. "Or maybe his marketing gurus make that shit up to get the teens slobbering."

"Yeah, right. The teens." I smirk at her. "It seems to be working pretty well on the college crowd too, from where I'm sitting."

"Cuz he's hotter than hell. If the devil made the perfect man to lure women into Hell, it's totally Trystan Scott. Mmm, mmmm. I'd follow his perfect ass anywhere."

I laugh at her. "You're so stupid. You would not."

"I would and I'd have no regrets, because that's the way I am. I see what I want and I take it and if that guy ever crosses my path, he's mine." She means every word of it. I almost envy her. Mel is so sure all the time, it's like she's never worried about anything.

I worry about everything.

CHAPTER 10

As Gabe pulls the car up to the hotel, my stomach dips. It feels like a bad omen, but I get out of the car anyway. I'm going to order bourbon and burn my tongue out of my mouth. I'm going to laugh and forget about things for a while.

As Mel and I walk across the lobby, several sets of male eyes fall on us. We take the elevator up to the restaurant and head for the bar. It's the middle of the week so it's not too crowded. Plus drinks here cost twice as much as anywhere else in the city, which drives away some people. I don't care. I love this place.

As Mel and I settle onto a couple of seats at the bar, a familiar voice speaks out behind me. The hairs on my neck prickle. Out of everyone, I never expected to see him again.

"Avery?" I turn around and see Peter Ferro, uh, Granz. He's standing there in a dark suit with his hair slicked back. Every strand is perfectly in place, which is the complete opposite of Sean's.

"Peter?"

Mel turns and glances at him, but says nothing. She flags down the bartender and orders for us while I talk to Sean's brother.

"I'm so glad to see you." He's smiling at me, but I have no idea why.

"Yeah, nice to see you too." For a second my stomach claws its way up my throat. I'm horrified that Sean is here with him, but as I glance around I know he's not. I don't know what he wants or what to say, so I smile at him and drop my gaze. I don't want to be reminded of last weekend.

Peter sits in the empty stool next to me. He opens his mouth a few times, laughs, and shakes his head. "I don't know how to say this, but I have to say it. Sean is an asshole—"

Mel smirks, "That's an understatement."

"So, you've met him too, then." Peter offers her a crooked smile and speaks to both of us. "Then you know how hard he is, how completely stoic and heartless he is?"

Mel nods. "You're preaching to the choir, baby."

Peter waits a beat and then asks me, "But when he's around you, something changes. I saw it at dinner the other night and it floored me. You changed him."

I nod and take the little shot glass in my hand. "I don't know about that."

"I do, and I have to ask why you let him walk away? It's none of my business—I know that—but you guys seemed happy together."

"I was his call girl, Peter. I didn't mean anything to him."

Peter smiles at me. It's just like Sean's, but less jaded, more hopeful. "You're wrong. You meant everything to him, but the guy has too much pride. He won't come back for you. You should go after him."

Mel laughs, like it's completely absurd. "Okay, crazy-man. And what makes you think that she's going to listen to you? How'd you even find her? Cuz I got my man Gabe over there and he'll come bust up your ass if you're stalking Avery—"

"Gabe's the one who told me she was here."

"Well, fuck. Does that man owe everyone a favor?" Mel pouts and looks into her empty shot glass. She taps the counter and orders another.

Peter glances at her and then back at me. "I'm not following you, I just had no way to contact you and I thought you'd want to know. I mean, if a woman was that bent out of shape over losing me, I hope someone would tell me. Especially if I thought she didn't care about me that much. Avery, whatever reason he gave you for leaving was weak. He regrets it, but I know he won't come back. He's too damn stubborn. It's not like Sean to admit when he's wrong, and he knows he screwed up with you."

I blink at Peter. Every thought in my head is saying he's lying, that there's no way Sean actually misses me. He would have called, he would have come back, he wouldn't have left if he actually wanted me. Pressing my lips together, I shake my head. He's wrong. I can't believe it. I laugh, but it sounds so bitter. "How could you possible know that?"

"Sunday's lunch was beyond weird. Sean and Sidney have been fighting non-stop since we've seen you. She basically told Sean he was an asshole and didn't deserve you. He said he knows that. It was the first thing they agreed on since they met. Sean thinks he screwed up so badly that there's no way to fix it, but there's always a way to fix it."

"No, not this." I twist the little cup between my fingers and stare at the amber liquid on the bar. "There's no way to repair this."

"Ah, I didn't realize you were the weak link in the relationship. My mistake. I naturally assumed it was Sean. Sorry to bother you." Peter gives me a look that says he thinks I'm a flake and turns away.

My spine straightens as offense hits me right between the eyes like a goddamn brick. "Hey!" I call after him, but Peter doesn't stop. I slip off the stool, take two steps, and grab his elbow. "I'm talking to you, Granz." Peter rounds on me with an infuriating smirk on his face.

"Oh, I'm sorry. I thought you were someone else. I thought you were the woman who was in love with my deranged brother. The older one. You're a bit too old for Jonathan."

"Don't talk to me like that! I'm not some little tramp that was following Sean around Long Island, because I had nothing better to do. I do love him! I still love him, but he doesn't want me. Why the hell would I chase after a guy who walked out on me?"

"Because he loves you and he's too damn proud to come back here after walking away. Because one of you has to be the grown-up here and get over yourself. Life's too short to live this way." Peter runs his hand over his hair. "Listen, in twenty years, when you look back, you'll know damn well that you could have gone after him, but you didn't. A lot of relationships end this way, but it didn't have to be yours. It takes two idiots to do this much damage. Just sayin'."

Can you say verbal bitchslap? Holy shit, is this the same shy guy that sat at the dinner table the other night. I can't believe he's talking to me like this. He doesn't know me, he doesn't know a damn thing about me. I'm bristling as he speaks, ready to assault him with a slew of sentences meant to cut his balls off, but Peter smiles and walks away before I open my mouth.

He calls back over his shoulder. "Don't be such a pussy, Avery. God knows you have balls if you can put up with Sean."

My mouth is hanging open. I'm not sure if that was a compliment or an insult. Mel is trying hard not to make a sound next to me. Her lips are caught between her teeth as she tries not to smile.

I glare at her. "What are you looking at?"

"Nothing. Just the best hooker in New York City, and apparently she has legendary brass balls." Mel's lips are twisted into a half grin. She looks ridiculous.

"He ruined my night."

"Uh-huh." Mel says, knocking back another shot.

"I don't need Sean."

"You don't."

My fingers clench into fists at my sides. I want to throw something. "Why'd he have to do that? Why'd his fucking brother have to show up and say that to me? Sean left me. We agreed to part ways. We don't want the same things."

"Nope, you don't."

"I'm better off without him."

Mel laughs and nods in agreement. "You are. You don't know him. He's a dick."

"Totally, he is. I don't need him at all. I don't…"

Mel slips off the stool and walks over next to me. She bumps into my shoulder, as she glances after Peter with me. "You think Mr. Twisted knows his brother told you all that shit?"

"No, Sean would hate that."

"So, what are you going to do?"

I turn to her and press my fingers to my heart, laughing lightly. "What, are you serious? You think I should go after Sean? Are you crazy? I don't want to be his mistress. Why would I go after him?" I stare at Mel like she's lost her mind.

A cat-like smile crosses her face. I swear to God, feathers are poking out of her lips when she says it, because she knows my reaction is going to be so incredibly bad. With her arms folded over her chest, tapping her glittery black nails, she says, "To ask him to marry you."

CHAPTER 11

I laugh. It's not real mirth—I'm so far from happy that I can't even describe the chronic meltdown that's occurring inside my mind. Take a polar ice cap and stick it in the microwave with some tin foil wrapped around it. That's what's going on inside my head. It's not just brains melting out of my ears that renders me speechless, it's the arcing—the frying of brain tissue—that actually prevents me from speaking. My eyes are dinner plates as my jaw shifts between tense and slack. I open it a few times while Mel knocks back her last drink and pays.

I swear to God, if I don't say something soon I'm going to lose my mind. The words that come out are a hodgepodge of sentences that are strung together rather incoherently. "That's a misconceived…so idiotic…array of insanity…" I press my lips together as my hands float up like I'm going to strangle something about waist-high. My hands tense, fingers flexing over and over again like I'm mental.

"Oh shit. I broke her." Mel laughs once and shakes her head at me. When I try to speak again and can't, she gives me a look. "I can't wait around for this shit, and I'm sure as hell not hanging out with you if you're going to be talking all fucked up like that. You sound like one of them people wandering around South Oaks." I scrunch up my face and glare at her – I'm not a mental patient. "Fine, be like that, but since our evening of fine conversation is obviously over, I'm heading home."

The car ride back to the dorm is quiet. The same thought goes through my mind over and over again. *I can't ask Sean to marry me. I can't.* I'm pretty sure that I haven't blinked for a while because my eyes sting.

Damn Peter, had to show up and say those things. It's not like things are easy for me. It's not like I can just stop school and skip work and go find Sean and propose. I can see the look on his face—that placid smile. He'd think I was joking and I couldn't stand that.

At the same time that thought bounces around in my head, another counters it. It's Peter's voice, saying that I'll regret it in twenty years—that I could fix this, if I tried.

Is that really what happened here? I didn't try hard enough? That's total shit. I did try. I never tried so hard to be with anyone in my life, and after everything that happened, it didn't matter because we aren't together anyway.

Sean needs randoms, a different woman to fuck every night. He doesn't need me.

Mel finally gets me talking by mentioning work. "I heard Black has a new dude picked out for you. The word from the herd is that he's a cowboy, decked out in all that Western shit. I bet he tries to ride you like a horse."

I smirk and glance at her out of the corner of my eye. "That would be a good night for me. Haven't you noticed? All my clients are insane? I'm starting to think Black is doing it on purpose. If this guy tries to brand me, I'll cut his balls off. Then Gabe can shove me in the trunk and drop me in the East River with cement shoes."

Mel snorts as she trudges up the stairs. "Gabe isn't the kind of guy that takes the time to make cement shoes. He does it with a bat and pushes you off a balcony. I bet you he covers his ass pretty good. No one can tell your brains were turned to pancake batter after they get scrambled on the sidewalk. Oh man, I'd kill for a Rooty Tooty Fresh and Fruity Stack right now."

"Nice segue. Disturbing and delicious."

She laughs as we stop in front of my door. I reach for the knob and flick my eyes up to hers. "Why'd you say it?" She had to know what it would do to me—how suggesting that I propose to Sean would commandeer every other thought in my head.

"Because you should. Play the whole game 'til the end. No regrets are at the end of that and you could use some steady right now. You second guess yourself too much. You have no idea how fucked up your life has gotten and that nutjob is the only guy that's turned your head, like ever.

"The question is, what kind of woman are you? Are you the kind to wait for some sappy guy to get down on his knee and ask for your hand in marriage? Because I don't think you are. I think you'd tell that guy no. I think you need the headcase as much as he needs you. You're both too stupid to admit it. Okay, I'm done playing Dr. Phil. My feet are killing me." Mel leans in suddenly and bangs her fist on the door. She shouts, "Get your sorry ass out of there right now, you pasty pastry or I'll bust your—"

The door flies open and Naked Guy gives me a sheepish look. He managed to pull his jeans on. A pair of boxers and a shirt dangle from his hand. He avoids Mel's gaze entirely and darts down the hall.

"You better run!" Mel yells after him. Then she looks at me and smiles. "Rodent removal complete. Unless you want me to throw your roommate out on her ass too?"

"I can hear you!" Amber shouts from inside the room.

"I don't give a shit, slutbag!" Mel's gaze narrows on the door, which I'm holding in my hand, half-opened, half-closed.

"Thanks Mel. I'm fine. I'll talk to you tomorrow."

But I don't see her on Thursday or Friday. I avoid Mel and Marty. I can't think and I have to figure this out on my own. The way I left things with Sean was good, well, it sucked but we were still on speaking terms. If I try to find him and propose, I risk messing that up and I don't know if I can bear it when he says no.

I fall asleep that night after tossing and turning way too long. Dreams come and are filled with storms and seawater that fills my lungs. Waves pummel me, but no one saves me. I drown and drift under the waves, with my lifeless body, into blackness.

CHAPTER 12

Saturday night comes and Mel knocks on my door while I'm getting ready for my new client—the cowboy. God, I hope he's not crazy. I've had enough mentally unstable men to last a lifetime. When I signed the contract, Miss Black was updating her files so I didn't see his picture, but I don't care. This doesn't matter. It's a means to an end. One more client, one more night of letting someone I don't care about use my body.

The weird thing is, since I saw Peter, I feel numb all over. I don't care about tonight or the guy. It's like someone dropped my sucky life into a vat of gel. Everything congealed and slowed.

The past few days feel like years. I've spent every free moment at my parent's grave, talking to a headstone. I wish my mother was here. I wish I could ask her what to do. Did she have to chase Daddy? Did they break up and get back together again? Is Peter right? I don't know and no matter how long I sit there, picking at the dead lawn and talking to her, there is no clarity.

Maybe I am a coward.

Mel doesn't wait for me to open the door. She busts into my room as I'm shimmying my dress over my head. It slips over my hair and I see her standing there, decked out for her client. "Ready to bang this guy?" She grins at me and hands me a white plastic bag.

I take it from her, after I zip my dress, and look inside. "Really?" There's a toy cap gun in there—the kind the Lone Ranger used, the kind you can't buy anymore. "Where'd you get these?"

"Antique shop."

"Shit, that makes me feel old. I played with these when I was a kid."

"Yeah, they're the real thing—asbestos and lead paint. They're metal, baby. Perfect for straddling some strapping young man." Mel grabs the guns and poses like Charlie's Angels before doing her Yosemite Sam routine.

My lips curl into a smile as I watch her. "You seriously need to keep those. I've never seen you so happy over some toy."

"I've got other toys that make me happy. We just don't share those. It's nasty."

"Mel!" I make a face and slip my heels on. "You're so gross."

"So, you got a new bracelet from Black?" I nod. "And you have no intention of skipping out on work and going after Love Buns?"

"No," I say, not meeting her gaze. "It's over. Just leave it alone."

"Fine. Well, have a fun fuck tonight. Use the guns in creative ways." She waggles her eyebrows at me.

I shove the guns back at her. "Seriously, keep them. You seem to have more uses in mind than I do, anyway."

She shrugs, "Fine by me. I have that kinky guy tonight. He'll love these."

———

By the time Gabe drops me off at the hotel, it's late. This client requested that I show up at his room at 9:00pm with a bottle of wine in hand. I approach the door in a daze. My heart doesn't even feel like it's beating anymore. Apathy has consumed me. I'm going to fuck this guy's brains out and go home.

I won't see Sean again.

It won't matter what I do with anyone else. It won't change the fact that I'm a hooker. It won't give me a chance with Sean. That's over. It's gone.

Raising my hand, I knock on the door and wait. Usually the guy is eager and the door flies open, but this guy makes me wait. I shift my weight to the other hip and consider knocking again, when I hear the metallic scrape of the lock. When the guy pulls the door open, he's standing in shadow. The lights in his room are off, except one that is directly behind him. He's taller than me, and well built. His sandy hair is tucked under a felt cowboy hat. The brim covers his face as he looks down at his boots.

"Hey," I say, not really looking past his clothing.

But when he speaks, I recognize him immediately. My stomach flips as I look up into those familiar brown eyes. "Hey yourself, little lady."

"Marty?"

**MORE BOOKS IN
THE FERRO FAMILY:**

SEAN FERRO
~THE ARRANGEMENT~

******

PETER FERRO GRANZ
~DAMAGED~

******

JONATHAN FERRO
~STRIPPED~

*****

THE ARRANGEMENT SERIES

*****

This story unfolds over the course of multiple short novels. Each one follows the continuing story of Avery Stanz and Sean Ferro.

To ensure you don't miss the next installment, text AWESOMEBOOKS to 22828 and you will get an email reminder on release day.

MORE ROMANCE BOOKS BY

H.M. WARD

DAMAGED

DAMAGED 2

STRIPPED

SCANDALOUS

SCANDALOUS 2

SECRETS

THE SECRET LIFE OF TRYSTAN
SCOTT

And more.

To see a full book list, please visit:

www.SexyAwesomeBooks.com/books.htm

CAN'T WAIT FOR H.M WARD'S NEXT STEAMY BOOK?

Let her know by leaving stars and
telling her what you liked about
THE ARRANGEMENT VOL. 8
in a review!

CPSIA information can be obtained
at www.ICGtesting.com
Printed in the USA
LVHW041153070419
613259LV00002B/459